D1444749

A warm greeting to
Korney Chukovsky in his heaven!

Rabén & Sjögren Bokförlag, Stockholm
http://www.raben.se
Translation copyright © 2000 by Rabén & Sjögren Bokförlag

Originally published in Sweden by Rabén & Sjögren under the title *Andrejs längtan*,
text copyright © 1997 by Barbro Lindgren, pictures copyright © 1997 by Eva Eriksson

Library of Congress catalog card number: 99-052905
Printed in Denmark
First American edition, 2000
ISBN 91 29 64756-8

Barbro Lindgren   Eva Eriksson

ANDREI'S SEARCH

Translated by *Elisabeth Kallick Dyssegaard*

R&S
BOOKS

Stockholm   New York   London   Adelaide   Toronto

Andrei is walking around the great city of St. Petersburg, searching
for his mother. Little Vova is with him. Little Vova is not looking for his
mother, because he doesn't have one.

Andrei used to have a mother. She wore a blue dress and had a barrette in her hair. And her voice was like a bell, the kind that sheep up in the mountains have around their necks.

She has been gone for so long that he can barely remember what her eyes looked like, whether they looked like small figs or like mulberries. And he has called out "Mama!" up and down many streets, and many mamas have stuck their heads out the windows, but none was his mama.

A long time ago, before he was born, he had lived inside her stomach, right under her heart. There he had his own room with a bed and a chair. And a staircase led to an attic where the moon shone in through the window.

He had had such a nice time there. There was a garden, too, with an apple tree and a plot of tiny lettuce. And behind the garden there was a store where everything was free, and a dog that was always happy.

But one day, when he was sitting on his little chair, thinking, she had suddenly given birth to him! He could never climb his staircase again or shop free-of-charge in his store. He could never again look at the moon through the window while listening to his mama's heart beat softly and gently. That was sad, because everything became much more difficult after he was born. He often longed to be back in his room with his bed and his chair and the handy staircase.

He asked his mama: "Why did you give birth to me?"

And his mother answered: "I wanted you to come out so we could have a nice time together."

But later, when they were supposed to have a nice time together,
she was suddenly gone! She was nowhere to be found. No matter
how much he called out, she didn't come.

Instead, two aunts came to get him. And when he asked where his
mama was, they said she had left. But they forgot to say where she
had gone. They brought him to a big house full of children. And there
were no mamas or papas there, only aunts.

"I want to go home to my little room under my mother's heart," said Andrei, sniffling. But they gave him a bed in a room that was full of boys and beds. And they said he should go to sleep, and then they closed the door.

Oh, how he longed for his little room and the bed and the chair! If only he were sitting in his little garden now, looking at the lettuce! He just had to cry.

Then he felt a hand on his cheek and heard a voice in the dark. "Why are you crying?"

It was little Vova in the next bed.

"I miss my mama," said Andrei, sniffling.

But Vova doesn't know what it means to miss someone; he has never seen his mama. Still, he understands that it hurts to miss someone.

And he softly strokes Andrei's cheek. They sigh many times and then they go to sleep.

When they wake up, it is morning. Vova puts his hand in Andrei's and they go to eat in the big, big room. Children are sitting in long rows, clattering with heavy spoons. Oh, how he longs for his own chair and his own spoon!

When they are finished eating, he whispers in Vova's ear:
"Come with me to look for my mama!"
Vova nods.
And they go out into the great city of St. Petersburg.

They come to a street with many houses. In every house there is a mama looking out the window.

"Mama!" Andrei calls out.

But none of the mamas is his. No one wears a blue dress. And none has a barrette in her hair.

Just then a trolley comes racing around the corner.

"A trolley just like that drove around the free
store all day long," says Andrei.

"Why is it running around here, then?" asks Vova.

"Because it is alive, of course!"

"But why is it shooting sparks?"

"It's angry. It wants to go lie down but it has to rush around.
That's why it's snorting so the sparks fly off it."

Vova feels sorry for the poor trolley that has to rush around even though it's tired.

Vova begins to get tired, too. His legs can't go much farther. He has to sit down on the sidewalk. Inside a yard, an apple tree is in bloom; it's so pretty.

"There's an apple tree just like that in my mama's garden," says Andrei. Vova has never seen an apple tree before.

"Why are there flowers on it?" he wonders.

"It wants to flower," says Andrei. "That's what trees want to do. My apple tree wanted to flower, too."

Vova wants to sit on the sidewalk for a long time.

"If your mother were here, she could carry you," says Andrei.

But Vova has no mother to carry him. Andrei has to carry him, instead.

"Who gave birth to you, then?" asks Andrei.

Vova looks at him with his kind eyes. "A little dog gave birth to me. But then she didn't want me. She only wanted puppies. So she gave me to the children's home." And Andrei sees that Vova does look quite a lot like a dog.

"You have a nose like the nose my dog had when I lived under my mama's heart. It was also called Vova!"

Vova looks happy.

"I bought pierogis in that free store."

"Were they good?" asks Vova. He is starting to look hungry.

"The best in St. Petersburg!"

Now Andrei is also beginning to be terribly hungry.

They get to the pierogi store. There are pierogis everywhere and the baker races back and forth between the oven and the counter.

"Is this a free store?" asks Andrei.

"What?"

"Is this a free store? We are hungry."

The baker grumbles. But he sees Vova's little dog face and stops.

"At precisely this second it is a free store," he says, and tosses them each a pierogi before he rushes back to the oven.

"You see!" says Andrei to Vova, who is very surprised.

They walk on.

Vova looks more and more like a dog. Andrei thinks his ears are more floppy now than they were this morning. And he pants in a doglike way when Andrei sets him down on the sidewalk.

Not too far away, a real dog is sitting, eyeing them seriously.

"It has the same eyes as you. That's probably your mama," says Andrei.

But Vova doesn't think so. She is much too small. He couldn't fit in her stomach! The dog looks at them for a long time. It wants to go home with them.

"But we have no home," says Andrei.

Then the dog starts to cry. Tears drip on the sidewalk.

"We'll take you home anyway," says Andrei.

The dog is very happy and follows them.

Soon it is thirsty.

They get to a river that runs through the city. The dog drinks and drinks. Its stomach gets bigger and bigger. Andrei thinks that soon Vova will be able to fit inside it. But Vova doesn't want to crawl in; he wants to be with Andrei and find his mama and the free store. Vova whispers something in the dog's ear.

"What are you whispering?" asks Andrei.

"Make some puppies for me," says Vova.

"What did she answer?"

"Yes, I'd be happy to."

"When are they coming?" asks Andrei.

"Tomorrow!"

Andrei thinks that's good, because by tomorrow he will definitely have found his mama. And then they can move into the house with the little garden.

A tugboat comes bobbing down the river.

"Why is it bobbing?" asks Vova.

"Because it's so happy, of course!"

"Why is it happy?" asks Vova.

"Because it can make clouds!"

Vova sees clouds coming out of its chimney and floating up to the sky.

"Behind my mama's garden there is also a boat that can make clouds," says Andrei.

Vova looks eagerly at him.

"You can have a boat like that when we find my mama!"

Then Andrei feels Vova's little hand in his own, and he sees that Vova's ears aren't flopping quite as much as before . . .

The dog follows them with its fat stomach. It is so happy it laughs all the time.
But it's beginning to get dark and they have to find Andrei's mama before it gets
pitch-dark. They pass many houses that look unfriendly. Andrei would never go
into such houses. But finally they get to a house that looks nice.

The staircase is just like Andrei's mama's. And the staircase leads up
to an attic with a window, which Andrei recognizes. And the moon is
shining just as he remembered!

"Mama!" Andrei calls out as loud as he can.

Through the window he sees the garden with the apple tree and
the small plot of lettuce.

"Mama! Mama!"

They hear a voice. It is like a bell, the kind that sheep have around their necks up in the mountains.

"Andrei! Here I am!"

And his mother comes through the garden in her blue dress with her barrette in her hair. She spreads her arms and he jumps to hug her. He is as happy as a child can be! It turns out just as he has dreamed for so long.

And Vova and the dog also come to live with her in the house with the garden. And the next day the dog gives birth to a whole bunch of puppies, and Andrei and Vova play with them every day.

Picture